WITHDRAWN

...independent reading!

STEP INTO READING® will help your child get there. The program offers five steps to reading success. Each step includes fun stories and colorful art or photographs. In addition to original fiction and books with favorite characters, there are Step into Reading Non-Fiction Readers, Phonics Readers and Boxed Sets, Sticker Readers, and Comic Readers—a complete literacy program with something to interest every child.

Learning to Read, Step by Step!

Ready to Read   Preschool–Kindergarten
• big type and easy words • rhyme and rhythm • picture clues
For children who know the alphabet and are eager to begin reading.

Reading with Help   Preschool–Grade 1
• basic vocabulary • short sentences • simple stories
For children who recognize familiar words and sound out new words with help.

Reading on Your Own   Grades 1–3
• engaging characters • easy-to-follow plots • popular topics
For children who are ready to read on their own.

Reading Paragraphs   Grades 2–3
• challenging vocabulary • short paragraphs • exciting stories
For newly independent readers who read simple sentences with confidence.

Ready for Chapters   Grades 2–4
• chapters • longer paragraphs • full-color art
For children who want to take the plunge into chapter books but still like colorful pictures.

STEP INTO READING® is designed to give every child a successful reading experience. The grade levels are only guides; children will progress through the steps at their own speed, developing confidence in their reading. The F&P Text Level on the back cover serves as another tool to help you choose the right book for your child.

Remember, a lifetime love of reading starts with a single step!

For my great-niece Avigail Felice —D.A.A.

For Paul —S.R.

Text copyright © 2018 by David A. Adler
Cover art and interior illustrations copyright © 2018 by Sam Ricks

All rights reserved. Published in the United States by Random House Children's Books, a division of Penguin Random House LLC, New York. Originally published in hardcover in the United States by Penguin Young Readers, an imprint of Penguin Random House LLC, New York, in 2018.

Step into Reading, Random House, and the Random House colophon are registered trademarks of Penguin Random House LLC.

Visit us on the Web!
StepIntoReading.com
rhcbooks.com

Educators and librarians, for a variety of teaching tools, visit us at
RHTeachersLibrarians.com

Library of Congress Cataloging-in-Publication Data is available upon request.
ISBN 978-0-593-43254-9 (trade) — ISBN 978-0-593-43255-6 (lib. bdg.)

Printed in the United States of America
10 9 8 7 6 5 4 3 2 1

This book has been officially leveled by using the F&P Text Level Gradient™ Leveling System.

Random House Children's Books supports the First Amendment and celebrates the right to read.

PASS THE BALL, MO!

by David A. Adler

illustrated by Sam Ricks

Random House 🏠 New York

"Who was our first president?"

Mo Jackson's teacher asks.

"George Basketball," Mo says.

Mo's teacher shakes his head.

"His name was George Washington,
not George Basketball."

"Oh," Mo says.

He's not thinking about presidents.

He's thinking about
basketball practice.

It's right after school.

At practice Coach Emma says,

"Mo, pass the ball."

Mo passes it to Gail.

It hits her knee and

bounces away.

"No, no!" Coach Emma says.

"Gail is taller than you.

Throw higher."

Everyone on the team

is taller than Mo.

Mo's team is the Bees.

Mo practices passing.

He throws the ball

against the wall.

"Throw it higher,"

Coach Emma tells him.

Mo throws the ball higher.

Coach Emma blows a whistle.

Tweet! Tweet!

Practice is done.

The Bees' first game is Saturday.

Mo walks home with his dad.

"I have to practice passing,"

he tells his dad.

Mo practices with his dad.

"Pass the ball," Mo's dad says.

His dad is even taller

than Gail.

Mo throws the ball high.

"Good pass," Mo's dad says.

It's Saturday.

"Eat a big breakfast,"

Mo's mother says.

"Basketball players need

to be strong."

One by one, Mo tosses blueberries
into his bowl of cereal.

Each time a berry lands in the bowl,

Mo says, "Yeah! Two points!"

He eats his breakfast.

His mom and dad take
him to the game.

They sit in the stands and watch.

The Bees are playing the Ducks.

Mo and Eve sit on the bench
and watch.

The Bees and Ducks run

from one end of the court

to the other.

They pass the ball.

They shoot the ball.

Sometimes it goes in.

Most times it doesn't.

Tweet! Tweet!

The first half is done.

The Ducks are winning 12 to 10.

The second half starts.

Mo and Eve are still on

the bench.

"I need to rest," Sam tells

Coach Emma.

"Go in," Coach tells Eve.

The game is almost over.

The score is Ducks 18,

Bees 18.

"I need to rest," Gail tells

Coach Emma.

"Go in," Coach tells Mo.

Mo runs onto the court.

"Hey, Little One," a Duck says to Mo.

"I'm not Little One. My name is Mo."

The Duck tells Mo, "And I'm Big Max."

Mo runs up and down the court.

Big Max runs with him.

Billy shoots the ball.

It hits the rim and rebounds to Mo.

"Pass it!" Coach Emma says.

"Pass it to me!" Janet says.

"Pass it to me!" Billy says.

Big Max is in the way.

"Here goes," Mo says.

He throws the ball high

over Max's head.

It is also over Janet's head.

It's over Billy's head, too.

The ball goes in the basket!

"YEAH!" Mo's parents and others cheer.

"Two points!" Coach Emma shouts.

Tweet! Tweet!

The game is over.

The Bees win 20 to 18.

The Bees carry Mo on their shoulders.
They carry him to his parents.

"Great shot," Mo's parents tell him.

"But I was trying to pass the ball,"

Mo says.

Coach Emma laughs.

"It was a very bad pass.

But your bad pass

won the game."

8